Sleepwalker

by J. Powell

illustrated by Paul Savage

Librarian Reviewer
Joanne Bongaarts
Educational Consultant
MS in Library Media Education, Minnesota State University, Mankato
Teacher and Media Specialist with Edina Public Schools, MN, 1993–2000

Reading Consultant
Elizabeth Stedem
Educator/Consultant, Colorado Springs, CO
MA in Elementary Education, University of Denver, CO

 **STONE ARCH BOOKS**
Minneapolis   San Diego

First published in the United States in 2007
by Stone Arch Books,
151 Good Counsel Drive, P.O. Box 669,
Mankato, Minnesota 56002.
www.stonearchbooks.com

Originally published in Great Britain in 2002
by Badger Publishing Ltd.

Original work copyright © 2002 Badger Publishing Ltd
Text copyright © 2002 Jillian Powell

The right of Jillian Powell to be identified as the author
of this work has been asserted by her in accordance
with the Copyright, Designs and Patent Act 1988.

Library of Congress Cataloging-in-Publication Data
Powell, Jillian.
      Sleepwalker / by J. Powell; illustrated by Paul Savage.
      p. cm. — (Keystone books.)
      Summary: When Josh moves in with his new stepbrother Tom, they
seem to have nothing in common, but when Tom begins sleepwalking, Josh
makes a frightening discovery.
      ISBN-13: 978-1-59889-095-2 (hardcover)
      ISBN-10: 1-59889-095-6 (hardcover)
      ISBN-13: 978-1-59889-245-1 (paperback)
      ISBN-10: 1-59889-245-2 (paperback)
      [1. Stepfamilies—Fiction. 2. Sleepwalking—Fiction. 3. Smuggling—
Fiction.] I. Savage, Paul, 1971–, ill. II. Title.
PZ7.P87755Sl 2007
[Fic]—dc22   2006004060

1 2 3 4 5 6 11 10 09 08 07 06

Table of Contents

Chapter 1

Almost There

"Almost there," Mom said.

Josh said nothing. He didn't want to be there.

He didn't see any more street lights. Just fields with cows in them.

Josh wanted to be back home, in the city.

"You'll be sharing a room with Tom," Mom said. "It will be like having a brother."

It will be horrible, Josh thought.

Josh had only met Brian's son, Tom, once, but he knew he was weird.

Oddly, they shared the same birthday, but that was all they had in common.

Tom didn't play on a soccer team. He didn't even know anything about PlayStation.

What did he do? He collected fossils. Josh thought it was pretty weird. Tom filled his bedroom with old rocks.

Josh closed his eyes. He tried to imagine his old room back home, except it wasn't home any more.

They were going to live with Brian and Tom in the middle of nowhere. Mom had said so and that was that.

Brian was waiting at the gate for them.

He kissed Mom. Then he slapped Josh on the back.

"Come on in, son," he said.

Josh pulled away.

"You're not my dad," he said.

"Josh!" Mom said.

Brian smiled at Mom.

"It's okay. Tom, why don't you show Josh his bedroom?" said Brian.

Tom put out his hand to take Josh's suitcase, but Josh held onto it.

He followed Tom up the stairs.

"We've got bunks," Tom said. "Do you want the top one?"

"Whatever," Josh said.

"Let's get all your stuff put away," Tom said.

Josh opened his suitcase. His hand slid into some slimy gunk.

The top of his hair gel bottle had come off. There was gel on his clothes. Tom must have done it, but when?

A few minutes later, Josh looked out the window. Tom was smiling and chatting with Mom and Brian.

It was all an act. Josh knew it. Tom didn't want him here any more than he wanted to be here.

Chapter 2

A Black Shape

In the morning, Josh slept late. Mom came in and woke him.

"Come on, Josh, we are all going down to the beach," she said. "You won't believe how close it is."

It was close all right. You just went out of the gate and there were the cliffs and the water.

Maybe the house will fall into the sea and we can go home, Josh thought.

Mom and Brian went ahead. Josh walked behind. Tom kept stopping and looking at the cliffs.

He came over to Josh with something in his hand. It was an old stone.

"Take a look," Tom said. The stone had lines on it.

"It's a fossil, millions of years old," Tom said. "You can have it if you want."

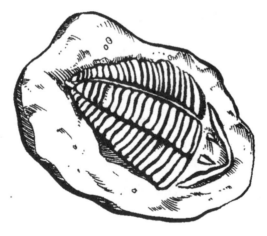

Josh looked at the stone, then he tossed it back on the sand.

"Did you find anything today?" Brian asked later. "Tom finds lots of things. Did you show Josh the shark's tooth, Tom?"

"I don't think he's interested," Tom said quietly.

That night, Mom, Brian, and Tom were watching television. Josh decided to go upstairs.

He climbed onto the top bunk and turned on the reading light. There was an odd sound.

Then something black shot across the room, just above his head. It swooped back towards him, flapping in his face. Josh felt its leathery wings.

Josh leaped down off the bunk and stood shaking. It was a bat.

The door opened and Tom appeared.

"You okay?" asked Tom.

Josh stood frozen.

"Oh, it's only a bat," Tom said.

"I don't care what it is, just get it out of here," Josh said.

He watched in horror. Tom went over and put his hand over the bat.

"They come down the chimney sometimes," Tom said.

I bet, Josh thought. This was another of Tom's tricks. He was so weird he probably had a pet bat.

Chapter 3

Moon Walking

Josh was bored. There was nothing to do and no one to hang out with. He tried to avoid Tom.

A few odd things had happened recently, like his watch. It was missing on the beach one day. He knew he was wearing it in the morning, but somehow he had lost it.

"Don't worry, we'll help you find it," Mom said.

Josh knew that was impossible. It could be buried in the sand, or even in the sea.

Then Tom turned up, with something in his hand. Josh's watch.

"I found it on the beach," he said, smiling.

"That's great, Tom!" Mom said. "Say thank you, Josh."

"See? I told you Tom could find anything," Brian said.

I'll bet he took it in the first place, Josh thought. Tom was fooling Mom and Brian, but he didn't fool Josh.

That wasn't all. Josh was lying in bed one night trying to sleep. Moonlight sliced across his bed like a white sword.

Josh felt the bunk beds shake. Tom was getting up.

"What's going on?" Josh asked.

Josh leaned over the side of the bunk. Tom didn't answer. He just got up and walked out of the room.

He was sleepwalking.

Chapter 4

Strange Things Happening

The next night, it happened again. Josh was lying in bed. Around midnight, he heard Tom getting up.

"Tom?" Josh asked

Tom didn't reply. He was getting dressed. Then he walked out of the room like a zombie.

This time, Josh decided to follow him. He pulled on a sweater and some shoes.

Tom was downstairs. He went to the back door, opened it, and walked out. Josh followed him.

It was dark. Tom walked along the path, then turned right at the gate. He was heading toward the cliffs.

Josh's heart began to race.

What if Tom fell? What if this was some trick to get him to the cliffs so Tom could push him over?

Tom kept on walking. He seemed to know where he was going. He stayed on the path. Josh followed him.

Then something caught Josh's eye. There was a jeep parked at the top of the cliff.

Then he saw something move on the beach. There were people down there, two of them, and a boat.

It was too dark to see clearly. Josh wondered if they were fishermen, but it wasn't a fishing boat. The jeep must be theirs. He could hear voices, but they were talking very quietly. Had Tom gone to meet them?

Suddenly Josh saw Tom coming back along the path. Tom walked past him back to the house. Josh followed, his head spinning.

Chapter 5

Smugglers

Josh didn't tell anyone what he had seen. He waited to see if Tom would sleepwalk again, but nothing happened until a month later.

Josh woke in the middle of the night. Tom's bed was empty. Josh swung out of bed and down the ladder. The back door was wide open.

Josh grabbed a pair of boots. He ran down the path.

Tom was ahead of him, walking along the cliffs. Then Josh saw the jeep, parked near the top of the cliff again.

He got a little closer.

This time, he could see better. There were three men.

One of them was taking something off the boat. The other two were standing together, talking in whispers. One man handed the second man an envelope. He put it in the inside pocket of his jacket.

Then they both went down to the boat and began helping the third man.

Suddenly, there were footsteps right behind Josh. He swung around, his heart thumping. It was Tom.

"Tom! Did you see them? I think they're smugglers," he whispered.

Tom was asleep. He just kept looking ahead as he walked back to the house.

Josh took another look. The men were coming up the cliff path toward the jeep. He thought he better go back to the house.

Chapter 6

Caught in the Act

The next day, Josh kept thinking about the smugglers. Tom said nothing. Josh was sure Tom didn't remember what happened, but something was making him sleepwalk. It was as if Tom knew something was going on.

That night, Josh lay awake and waited. After midnight, he heard Tom get up.

Josh followed him out of the house and along the cliff path. There was the jeep. There were the men, on the beach by the boat.

Josh needed to get closer. He needed evidence. A steep path, just by the jeep, led to the beach. Josh began to creep down the path.

The men were unloading the boat.

"These are good," he heard one say.

"The best," another said.

So that was it! They were art smugglers.

Josh was watching them closely when his foot slipped. A stone bounced down the cliff face.

The men looked up, searching the cliffs with their eyes.

One of the men pointed at Josh and they began running up the path.

Josh's heart was pounding. He had to get out of there. He ran up the path and back toward the house.

The men were getting closer. He looked back and there was Tom, slowly walking along the path.

There was a roar as the jeep engine started up.

The jeep was heading straight at Tom!

Chapter 7

Close Call

"Tom!" Josh shouted.

Tom just kept walking slowly. Josh had to wake him up.

The jeep was catching up to Tom. Stones flew from its wheels as it went toward him. Its headlights were blinding.

They were going to kill him.

"Tom! Look out!" Josh shouted.

Josh began to run toward Tom. The
jeep roared closer and closer.

Josh watched in horror as Tom
vanished over the cliff.

The jeep braked less than a yard
from the edge. Two men got out and
looked down over the cliff.

Then they got back into the jeep and drove away fast.

Josh was shaking. He raced toward the cliff edge and looked down.

A dark shape caught his eye. It was just a rock. The beach was empty.

Suddenly he heard a beeping sound. There it was again. It sounded like a watch.

"Tom, Tom! Are you there? Are you okay?" Josh asked.

Josh lay down on the ground. He hooked his feet around a clump of grass. Then he pushed forward so he was leaning right over the edge.

There was a ledge hidden under the cliff edge. There was Tom, barely holding on. He looked scared.

"Okay, Tom," Josh said. "It's me, Josh. Just hang on, and we'll get you out of there."

Josh reached down with both hands.

"Grab on to me," he told Tom. "I won't let you go."

Josh pulled Tom to safety.

Chapter 8

Operation Sleepwalker

"Breakfast! Josh! Tom!"

Josh's mom stood on the stairs. She couldn't believe her ears. Josh and Tom were talking together like best friends.

"Do you hear this, Brian?" Josh's mom asked.

"They must have found something in common," Brian said with a smile.

"Can't stop for breakfast, Mom," Josh said.

The two boys disappeared quickly through the front door.

They were on their way to the coast guard. They knew they had stumbled on to some serious stuff.

Josh had remembered the jeep's license plate number. He knew there were three men. He knew the dates the boat had come in.

"That's good," the coast guard had told him. "That gives us time to plan."

That's how Operation Sleepwalker had started.

Josh and Tom were at the heart of it. They were there when the police arrested the men. The boys had uncovered a major smuggling operation.

* * *

"If I start sleepwalking again, will you stop me?" Tom asked.

"No way," Josh said. "After all, you never know where it will lead!"

About the Author

Jillian Powell started writing when she was very young. She loved having a giant pad of paper and some pens or crayons in front of her. She made up newspaper stories about jewel thieves and spies. Jillian's parents still have her early stories, complete with crayon illustrations!

About the Illustrator

Paul Savage works in a design studio. He says illustrating books is "the best job." He's always been interested in illustrating books, and he loves reading. Paul also enjoys playing sports and running. He lives in England with his wife and their daughter, Amelia.

Glossary

arrest (uh-REST)—to take hold of someone by the power of the law.

avoid (uh-VOID)—to keep away from

coast guard (KOHST gard)—a military group that guards the coast of a country and helps boats and ships in trouble

evidence (EV-uh-duhnss)—something that shows proof

fossil (FOSS-uhl)—the remains or trace of a plant or animal that lived long ago, found in rocks and the earth's crust

gel (JEL)—a jellylike substance

ledge (LEJ)—a flat space like a shelf in the side of a cliff

smuggler (SMUHG-ler)—a person who moves something secretly and illegally

vanished (VAN-ishd)—disappeared

zombie (ZOM-bee)—a person who acts without knowing it, or without being aware of their surroundings

Discussion Questions

1. There are lots of stories about people who sleepwalk and about what they do while walking around in the middle of the night. Do you know of anyone who walks in his or her sleep? Talk about what they do and what the people who live with them do.

2. Why didn't Tom and Josh like each other at first? Explain.

3. Why did Tom's sleepwalking occur on the same nights that the smugglers were out? Did he know what was going on? Explain your thinking.

Writing Prompts

1. Josh thought that Tom was playing tricks on him at the beginning of the story. What do you think about playing tricks on other people? Write about a trick that you played on someone or that someone played on you. What happened? How did you feel about it?

2. The parents in this story did not seem to know that Tom was a sleepwalker. Write about what they would have done if they did know.

Also by J. Powell

5010 Calling

The year is 5010. Beta sets up a thought-link with Zac from the year 2000 to help with his history project. Then Beta gets Zac into trouble.

The Reactor

When Joe and his friends are locked out of The Reactor, an abandoned building they had claimed as their own, they set out to uncover the sinister activities of the mysterious new owners.

Other Books in This Set

Alien Abduction
by Jonny Zucker

When Shelly and Dan are abducted by Zot the alien, they teach him about the ways of earthling teenagers. Hopefully they can convince Mr. Tann of their story before they end up in big trouble!

Space Games
by David Orme

Todd's travels across the universe are no match for a good game of soccer. When a soccer field is built aboard his starship, he dreams of leading his team to universal glory.

Internet Sites

Do you want to know more about subjects related to this book? Or are you interested in learning about other topics? Then check out FactHound, a fun, easy way to find Internet sites.

Our investigative staff has already sniffed out great sites for you!

Here's how to use FactHound:

1. Visit *www.facthound.com*

2. Select your grade level.

3. To learn more about subjects related to this book, type in the book's ISBN number: **1598890956**.

4. Click the **Fetch It** button.

FactHound will fetch the best Internet sites for you!